TJARDA REAVY

Fast Food
Maniac

ISBN: 978-1-4866-0870-6

Word Alive Press
131 Cordite Road, Winnipeg, MB R3W 1S1
www.wordalivepress.ca

Library and Archives Canada Cataloguing in Publication

Reavy, Tjarda, 1947-, author
        Fast food maniac / Tjarda Reavy.

Issued in print and electronic formats.

ISBN 978-1-4866-0870-6 (pbk.).--ISBN 978-1-4866-0871-3 (pdf).--
ISBN 978-1-4866-0872-0 (html).--ISBN 978-1-4866-0873-7 (epub)

        I. Title.

PS8635.E24F38 2015   jC813'.6   C2015-900784-4
                                              C2015-900785-2

To my husband,
who loves fast food.

Once upon a time, in a city near you, lived two gangs. They were known as the Fast Food Gang and the Slow Food Gang. Let me introduce them to you. The members of the Fast Food Gang were maniacs. *Maniac* means being crazy about something. They were crazy about fast food.

Can you guess what fast food is? Fast foods are things like French fries, hot dogs, tacos, chips, hamburgers…and I'm sure you could name many more. If not, then ask your mom and dad. Now why do we call it fast food? Fast food is usually any food that has little nutrition and generally lots of calories. Usually, when you go to a fast food restaurant, you would not think of ordering vegetables or fruits.

Now, slow food is, of course, the exact opposite of fast food. Slow food is usually food made from good healthy ingredients with fewer calories. The members of the Slow Food Gang were maniacs about slow food.

So that is how the names of these gangs came about.

The Fast Food Gang took the roads going through cities so that they would be close to places where they could buy their food three times a day. They thought they were being smart and saving time by having their food made fast in restaurants. Can you guess what they were eating? Many things slowed this gang down. Sometimes they had to stop and wait for traffic lights. In many towns, they had to stand in lineups at restaurants. Often they would have to wait for the food to be cooked.

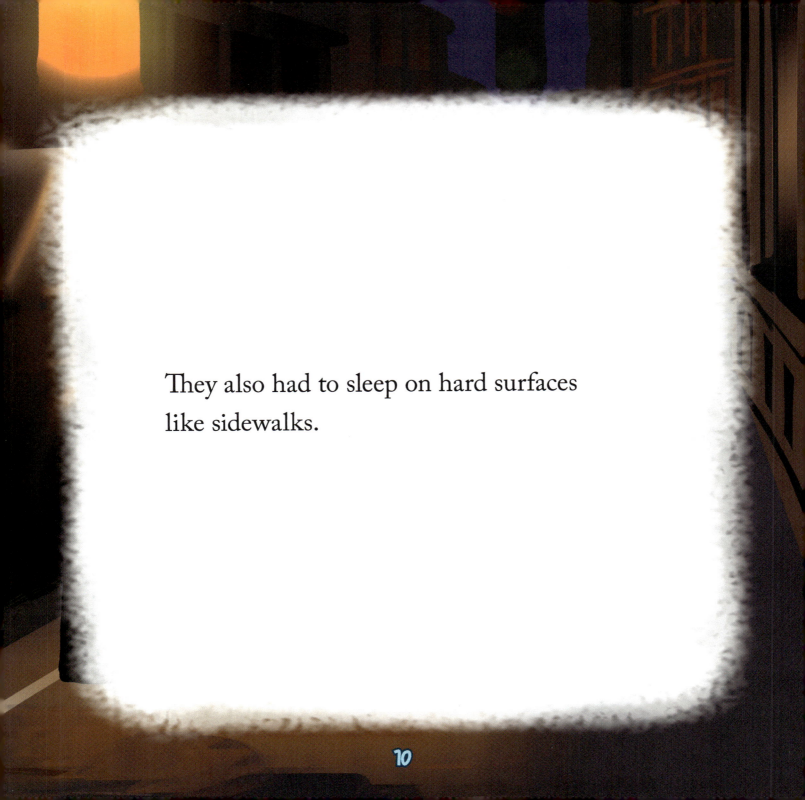

They also had to sleep on hard surfaces like sidewalks.

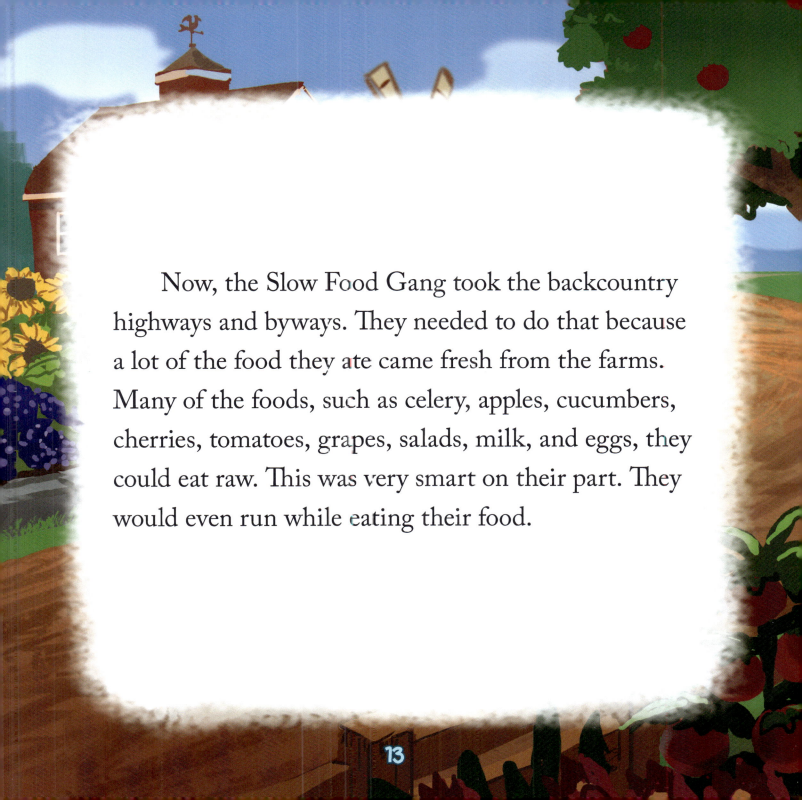

Now, the Slow Food Gang took the backcountry highways and byways. They needed to do that because a lot of the food they ate came fresh from the farms. Many of the foods, such as celery, apples, cucumbers, cherries, tomatoes, grapes, salads, milk, and eggs, they could eat raw. This was very smart on their part. They would even run while eating their food.

There was little traffic on the country roads and lots of open space where they could sleep comfortably in the grassy fields.

As a result, the Slow Food Gang members were way ahead of the Fast Food Gang at the end of the race, finishing the race first. They came in running and dancing, but the Fast Food Gang members came in walking slowly and looking very tired. Some were even sick.

The city had a celebration, but the members of the Fast Food Gang were too tired and sick to join in, and so they went to bed.

The two gangs never argued again.

From that moment on, the Fast Food Gang members respected the Slow Food Gang members. And that was not all…healthy slow food became popular in their cities.

These gangs would constantly argue about who ate the best food, the food that would make the eater strong and able to run fast. These two gangs finally came to a solution that would bring an end to their fighting and arguing. The solution was to have a long-distance run around the world. Both gangs took up this challenge.

Gang members packed their backpacks with only a change of clothing.

The start and finish line for the race would be each gang's hometown. They agreed that when they would come to bodies of water they would rent boats. Also, they must take time to eat and sleep, even if this would slow them down. Each had to make the trip around the middle of the earth, which is called the equator, and it is always hot there. Besides sleep, all gang members would need to eat and this would make the difference on how fast they could travel and complete their journey.

Ready, set, go . . .

When you sit down to eat…consider carefully
what is before you.

—Proverbs 23:1 (BBE)

Other Books by Tjarda Reavy

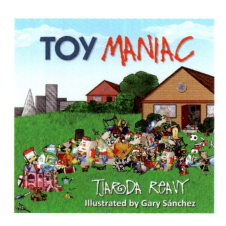

TOY MANIAC

978-1-77069-725-6

Meshach, Mateo, Malachi and their sister Melanie love to play with their toys! But what happens when they have so many that there is a mountain of toys in the basement? Will they fill the whole house? Find out how four siblings learn to share with others, and gain a valuable lesson about giving.

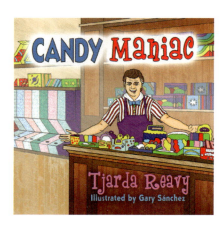

CANDY MANIAC

978-1-4866-0309-1

Everyone loves candy, but too much of it can be a very bad thing! Kevin, the caring owner of the first candy store in Fruit City, knows this all too well. Learn what happens when he and the mayor change the name of their city twice and save the people from eating too much candy.

CPSIA information can be obtained
at www.ICGtesting.com
Printed in the USA
444108LV00001B/2